To Noli and Jordy, with love from Mom — H.L.P.

To the Meyers family, with love and thanks! — B.C.

Text copyright © 1999 Hope Lynne Price.
Illustration copyright © 1999 Bryan Collier.
All rights reserved. No part of this book may be reproduced or transmitted in any form
or by any means, electronic or mechanical, including photocopying, recording, or by any
information storage and retrieval system, without written permission from the publisher.
For information address Hyperion Books for Children, 114 Fifth Avenue,
New York, New York 10011-5690.
Printed in Hong Kong.

First Edition
1 3 5 7 9 10 8 6 4 2

This book is set in Gill Sans 48/60.

Library of Congress Cataloging-in-Publication Data
Price, Hope Lynne.
These hands/Hope Lynne Price; illustrated by Bryan Collier—1st ed.
p.   cm.
Summary: Illustrations and simple text describe some of the many things hands can do.
ISBN 0-7868-0370-3 (trade)—ISBN 0-7868-2320-8 (lib.)
[1. Hand—Fiction. 2. Stories in rhyme.] I. Collier, Bryan, ill. II. Title.
PZ8.3.B7276Th 1999
[E]—dc21 99-19157

These Hands

Written by **Hope Lynne Price** • *Illustrated by* **Bryan Collier**

Jump at the Sun

HYPERION BOOKS FOR CHILDREN
New York

These hands
can touch.
These hands
can feel.
These hands
create.
These hands
can build.

These hands
can reach.
Can stretch.
Can teach.

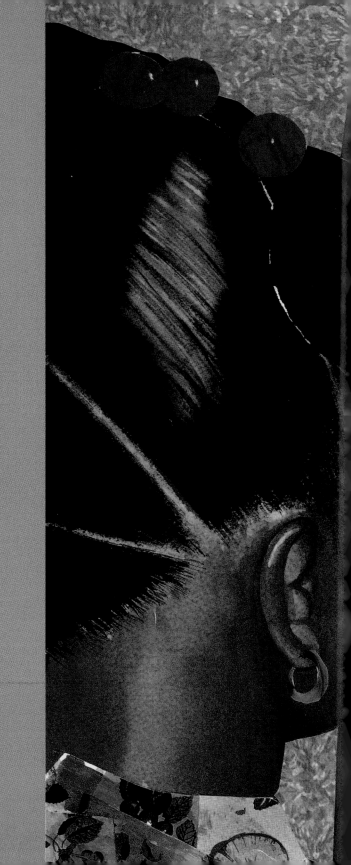

These hands
can hug.
Can pat.
Can tug.

These hands
can squeeze.
Can tickle.
Can please.

These hands
can hide
something
inside.

These hands
can write.
Can fly a kite.

These hands
can talk.
Help Grandma
walk.

These hands
can read.
Can share.
Can feed.

These hands
can shake
you wide
awake.

These hands
can pray.
Can clap.
Can play.

Can sow the
seeds
for a brighter
day.

Can sow the
seeds
for a brighter
day.